THE SEASONS

Summer

BARRON'S

Between spring and fall there
is a very hot season.
It is called ...

3

When it is *hot,* whatever is wet becomes dry very quickly. The water on your swimsuit just disappears !

It is the season when school is out, but not everybody has a *vacation,* do they ?

Many people go away to spend their vacation. How many ways can you travel?

We can go to the *beach* and build sand castles or make shell necklaces, learn how to swim, or play in the waves.

When you are in the country, if you look carefully, you can see a lot of small *animals:* dragonflies, grasshoppers, centipedes, ladybugs, mosquitoes, flies, spiders ... Can you hear the noise they make?

Wherever you go, you should protect yourself from the direct *sun*, especially if you have a fair complexion.
Can any of these things be of help?

16

It is the time for warm nights. Have you noticed how many *stars* there are in the sky?

With the heat, even plants dry up;
that's why we often have to *water*
flower and vegetable gardens
if it does not rain.

23

24

Almost all tomatoes in the *garden* are ready to eat. What else would you eat from this vegetable garden?

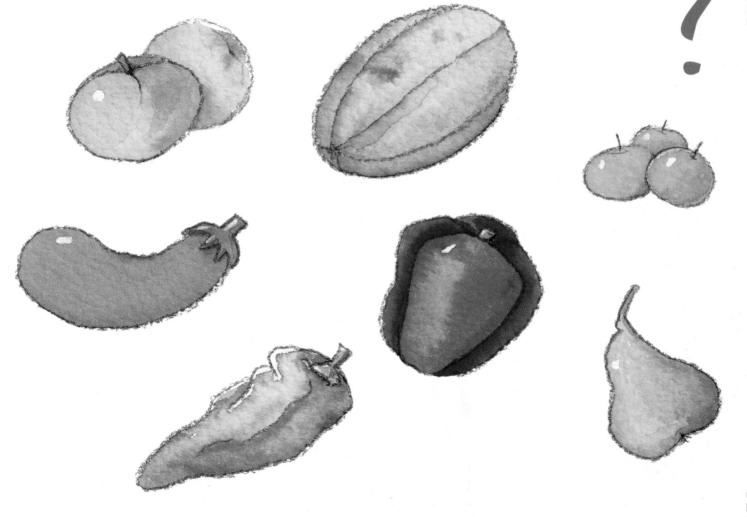

26

Cereals are harvested before the fall rain arrives. They are used to make bread, macaroni, and pies. Delicious!

Summer is just perfect for building
cabins, playing, dancing, and having
parties *outdoors.*
It is a very entertaining season !

Let's take a look underwater

With this viewer you will be able to see underwater easily. You need a plastic bottle, a plastic bag (the more transparent, the better), some water-resistant adhesive tape, and scissors.

1. Cut off the bottom part of the bottle.
2. Cover the cut-off end with the plastic bag.
3. Hold the plastic bag in place with the adhesive tape.

Now you can see underwater!

1   **2**   **3**

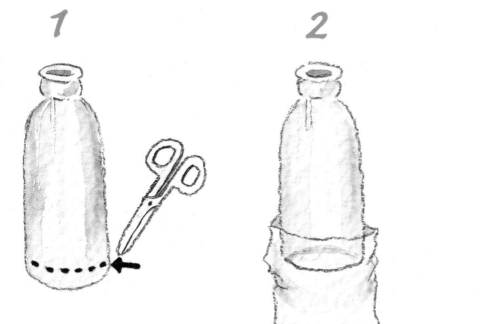

A mobile

Got a wooden stick, some thread, and cardboard?
You can make a very funny mobile. Here is how.
Draw some fish, starfish, and octopuses on the
cardboard. Now paint them and cut out the figures.
Make a tiny hole close to the upper side of each
figure and, with a little help from a grownup,

you can now hang them
from the stick!

A paper boat

Follow the instructions we provide and you will learn how to make a great paper boat. Let's see if you are able!

Then you can teach your friends how to do it!

1

2

3

4

1

3

5

6

7

8

9

10

A vacation schedule

It is summertime and you do not go to school, but you can review the things you do in one day just the same. You only need to draw a clock and write the hour. Next to it write everything you have done during that hour. Special and important activities can go in a brighter color to stand out from the rest.

See how many things you can do in just one day!

Guide for the parents

Sooner or later, summer arrives

Summer starts June 21st and finishes September 21st. It is hot and the days are very long. As in every season, on the first day of summer we can go over the summer months and indicate special days, such as celebrations, the beginning of vacations, and so forth. According to the children's age, we can use summer-related sayings, proverbs, or songs. Sometimes it will be the children who will teach us.

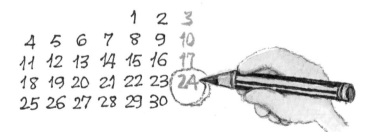

Not everybody has a vacation

School is closed in the summer and children go on vacation. Many people also have a vacation from work. However, many other people work all summer long. We can talk about professions linked to vacation time: waiters and waitresses, cooks, swimming pool and beach lifeguards, adventure sports leaders . . . We can also talk about other people with special work schedules, such as radio broadcasters, firefighters, doctors, sanitation and public utility workers, bakers … There are quite a lot!

Harvest time

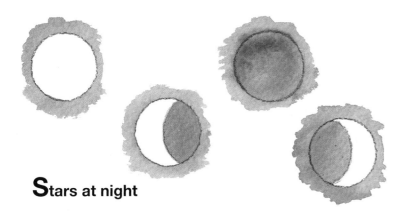

There are no vacations in the country either—it is harvest time. If you go away from town in the summer it is easy to see fields ready for harvest. You can explain that harvest was done by hand before. In some places there was so much work that people from other places had to come and help to finish the harvest on time. It is still like this in many regions, although machines are used more and more to do the work. However the harvest is done, it is always a good time for a big celebration when it is finished.

Stars at night

Summer is a good time to watch the sky at night: shooting stars, constellations, planets, and the moon. The latter is a good subject to start with; it moves around the Earth and it looks different according to the time of month: we can see a full moon, new moon, crescent moon, or waning moon. With a full moon there is so much light that we can take a walk at night without a flashlight. Stars are suns like ours, or even bigger, but they are so far away they just look like bright spots. The distance is so great no ship has been invented yet to reach the stars. The universe is simply immense!

Things may be lukewarm, cold, or hot

It is hot in summer, cold in winter. Let's touch cold things, for example an ice cube, and warm things, for example warm water. Some things are neither hot nor cold; they are lukewarm. Older children will understand the explanation that things freeze when it is extremely cold, for example an ice cube or snow. And when it is very, very, hot, water evaporates. That's why wet clothes from the laundry get dry. Water does not disappear but becomes vapor, which we cannot see, and it goes up toward the sky, where it forms part of clouds.

Making a schedule

The children will need your help to make a schedule. As usual, it is important to let the boy or girl choose all colors and shapes. You only need to supervise and let them make the decisions. Teach them how to tell the time and show them the many things we do in just one day. Smaller children may be prompted to make a clock (a circle with numbers where you indicate). As usual, adapt the activities to the child's age but value the child's autonomy.

Original book title in Catalan: *L'Estiu*
© Copyright Gemser Publications S.L., 2004.
C/Castell, 38; Teià (08329) Barcelona, Spain (World Rights)
Tel: 93 540 13 53
E-mail: *info@mercedesros.com*
Author: Núria Roca
Illustrator: Rosa Maria Curto

First edition for the United States and Canada (exclusive rights), and the rest of the world (non-exclusive rights) published in 2004 by Barron's Educational Series, Inc.

Address all inquiries to:
Barron's Educational Series, Inc.
250 Wireless Boulevard
Hauppauge, New York 11788
http://www.barronseduc.com

ISBN-13: 978-0-7641-2735-9
ISBN-10: 0-7641-2735-7
Library of Congress Catalog Card Number 2004101340

Printed in China
9 8 7 6 5 4

THE SEASONS

Summer